W9-BTT-965

A Dragon Moves In

Moves In

written and illustrated by

Lisa Falkenstern

Marshall Cavendish Children

Marshall Cavendish Corporation
99 White Plains Road
Tarrytown, NY 10591
www.marshallcavendish.us/kids

Library of Congress Cataloging-in-Publication Data

Falkenstern, Lisa.
 A dragon moves in / written and illustrated by Lisa Falkenstern. — 1st ed.
    p. cm.
 Summary: When Rabbit and Hedgehog bring home a newly-hatched dragon they all have a wonderful time together, but soon the dragon baby grows too big for their house.
 ISBN 978-0-7614-5947-7 (hardcover) —
 ISBN 978-0-7614-5995-8 (ebook)
 [1. Rabbits—Fiction. 2. Hedgehogs—Fiction. 3. Dragons—Fiction. 4. Dwellings—Fiction.] I. Title.

PZ7.F19445Dr 2011   [E]—dc22   2011001122

The illustrations were rendered in oil on board.

Book design by Vera Soki
Editor: Margery Cuyler

Printed in China (E)
First edition
10 9 8 7 6 5 4 3 2 1

To Ken—I never could have done this book without you
—L.F.

*I*t was spring . . .
so Rabbit and Hedgehog
packed a picnic and settled in a sunny spot.
As they nibbled on ginger cookies,
something strange happened.

RUMBLE!

Rabbit dropped his teacup and shouted,
"This rock is shaking my tail!
I think we're having an earthquake!"

CRACC

"Earthquake?" said Hedgehog.
"Don't you mean EGG-QUAKE?
A baby dragon egg-quake?"

"A baby dragon!" Rabbit said.
"What do we do now?"

"Let's take him home," said Hedgehog.

So that's exactly what they did.

The three friends had lots of fun.

Morning . . .

noon . . .

and night.

But soon,
Rabbit and Hedgehog
realized there was
a growing
problem.

Their friend was getting **BIGGER**...

and BIGGER . . .

until one day he became
so **BIG**, he got . . .

"He can't get out!" cried Rabbit.
"What shall we do?"

"I have an idea," said Hedgehog.
"Tug on his nose!"

So Rabbit tugged and tugged
and tugged some more.

"Oh no! He's still stuck!" cried
Rabbit.

"I have a better idea," said Hedgehog. "Pull on his tail!"

So Rabbit pulled and pulled and pulled some more.

Suddenly . . .

BOOOOOM!

"Uh-oh, Rabbit!" said Hedgehog. "I think you pulled *too* hard."

"Oh dear," Rabbit said. "Look at our house. What do we do now?"

"I have a GREAT idea," said Hedgehog. "Let's build . . .

. . . a new house!"

"And make it big
enough for all of us,"
said Rabbit.

So they all worked
together . . .

until their new house was finished.

"Now can we go back to having fun?" asked Rabbit.

"You have the *best* idea yet," said Hedgehog.

And that is exactly . . .

what they did.